To Lowell, Lee, and Chelsea

Text and illustrations copyright © 2008 by Mo Willems.
ELEPHANT & PIGGIE is a trademark of The Mo Willems Studio, Inc.

All rights reserved. Published by Hyperion Books for Children, an imprint of Disney Book
Group. No part of this book may be reproduced or transmitted in any form or by any means,
electronic or mechanical, including photocopying, recording, or by any information storage
and retrieval system, without written permission from the publisher. For information address
Hyperion Books for Children, 125 West End Avenue, New York, New York 10023.
Printed in the United States of America
Reinforced binding

First Edition, June 2008
20 19 18 17 16 15 14 13 12
FAC-034274-16259

Library of Congress Cataloging-in-Publication Data on file.
ISBN: 978-1-4231-0961-7
Visit www.hyperionbooksforchildren.com and www.pigeonpresents.com

I Love My New Toy!

An ELEPHANT & PIGGIE Book

By Mo Willems

Hyperion Books for Children/New York
AN IMPRINT OF DISNEY BOOK GROUP

Hi, Piggie!
What are you
doing?

4

8

I love
throwing toys.

Here.
Try it.

Zip!

Nice throw.

Thanks.

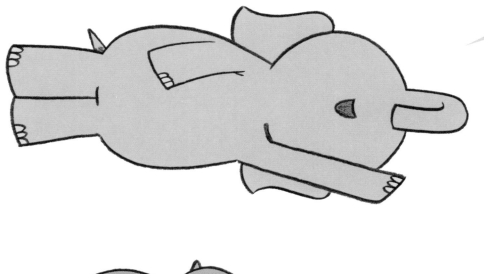

Turn

Here it comes!

ZOOM!

Turn

I broke your toy.

You broke my toy.

25

My new toy
is broken!

And YOU broke it!

AAAAH!

AAAAH!

Cool!

You have a
break-and-snap toy.

SNAP!

Enjoy!

BREAK!

BREAK!

SNAP!

No.

51

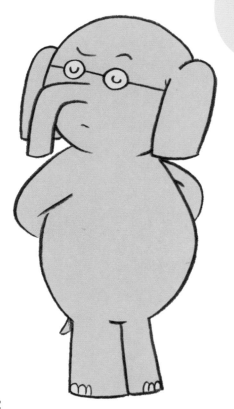

You do not want to play with my new toy?

Friends are more fun than toys.

Have you read all of Elephant and Piggie's funny adventures?